LITTLE PEST

ONCE UPON A BITE #1

CHARITY PARKERSON

Punk & Sissy Publications

COPYRIGHT

—Warning: This book is intended for readers over the age of 18. Some of my books contain allusions to past abuse and trauma. I try to have nothing triggering on page and treat every situation with care.

CONTENTS

INTRODUCTION

DRACO IS THE OLDEST vamp around. Tate is the newest and possibly the most annoying. They're the perfect pair.

As one of the oldest living vampires, Draco has seen a lot of history. He's also extremely powerful. With that power comes an allure that draws younger supernaturals to him like flies, hoping for a taste of his... expertise. Draco wants none of that. He lives a quiet life as a magician at a casino in Vegas. It's a fun gig for a retired vamp with no real responsibilities left to his name. Then Tate flies into his life. Now nothing is the same.

Tate is a little hapless. He's a little everything, actually. In fact, that pretty much sums up his personality. He's a Little. At least, he was before some dude bit him in a nightclub and now Tate is stronger than ten men, can control minds, and turn into a bat. He has no clue how he's doing any of that. No one taught him how to be a vampire. In fact, he doesn't know how to survive. Without Draco's help, he won't. If it means Tate has to make a pest of himself to get Draco to notice him and teach him the how-tos of his new life, then so be it. Falling in love, that was just another one of Tate's little mistakes, but it might be his best one yet.Lit

Little Pest is the first book in Charity Parkerson's Once Upon a Bite series.

These books are meant to be short, fun paranormal romps to brighten your day.

CHAPTER ONE

THE THRUM OF LOUD music pulsed in Tate's ears. Darkness enveloped him as he headed down the alleyway toward a hidden entrance. A small voice in the back of Tate's mind warned him this was crazy. He knew nothing about the nightclub other than what his friend Cosmos had told him. Hell, Tate had never even been sure Cosmos was the guy's real name, even though they had been friends for close to six months. But Cosmos said this was where people went to lose themselves and Tate desperately needed that tonight. Tate hoped he wasn't wrong.

He gave his assigned password to the gigantic doorman whose muscle nearly blocked out the entire doorway, and then held his breath. The door swung wide. Eerie music spilled out, drawing Tate inside as the bouncer stepped aside. His eyes widened at the sight that met him. Nude men danced in cages while other men watched. Couples of every spectrum of the rainbow took advantage of the darkly lit club, doing things most people kept private. None of that was what held Tate captivated. There was a spot for the Littles tucked in the back. Tate hugged his teddy bear to his chest and padded over to the giant playpen, more than a little excited to join the fun. He swore he felt greedy gazes as they followed his every move.

Tate fought the urge to pull the hood of his unicorn onesie tighter so no one could see his face. Even though he had been to fetish clubs in the past, this was his first time here and his first time going to one alone. Tate felt more exposed than he expected. He didn't make it to the playpen. A large body pressed against his back. A muscular arm locked around his waist.

"Are you lost, poppet?"

The English accent was thick but old in a way Tate couldn't describe. He almost reminded Tate of a pirate or the bad guy someone met in an alley in an old movie about London.

Tate turned his head. His breath caught. Light blue eyes caught the club's barely existent light and reflected it back—like a predator. A hint of fangs showed when the man smiled at Tate's open surprise. Tate swallowed. This was a fetish club. Nothing was real here. Everything was a game. He needed to remember that. "I'm not lost." The man's eyes mesmerized him. He terrified Tate, but he also possessed an allure Tate couldn't deny. Tate heard himself admitting more than he liked. "I am looking for something, though."

"Oh? Perhaps I can help."

Tate licked his parched lips. Fear and curiosity mixed to stop him from crying out for help. He squared his shoulders. "I'm looking for a daddy."

A woman materialized at the man's side. They were identical. They matched in every way, except for their sex. One second, she hadn't been there and the next—she was. Tate didn't know if his terror made it seem that way or if she had truly just appeared from thin air. Her mocking laughter wasn't something he imagined, though. That was very real. "This is the one, Ollie. Make it quick." Her gaze swept down his body in a way that made his skin crawl and his heart drop. "But not too quick. I like it when they cry."

Tate held his teddy bear tighter. He suddenly wished he hadn't been quite so brave about coming here alone tonight. Cosmos had been adamant this place was safe for people like him. Now, it looked like Tate would die here and no one would even look for him.

Find Draco.

The words brushed his mind as the darkness enveloped him, and control left his body. Tate didn't know who said them or if it had merely been a terror dream. Not that it mattered, since he was dead. How odd to think of a complete stranger in his last moments. Not that anyone he knew in real life was any better. Still, no one knew how much he wished life had been kinder, because his death was incredibly cruel.

CHAPTER TWO

APHELION HOTEL AND CASINO had been Draco's home since its opening in nineteen twenty. Located near the south end of the strip, he had a spectacular view of the pyramid-shaped casino and the place that vaguely reminded him of the renaissance years. Draco only got to see them at night, but he imagined that was when they were at their best anyhow. Millions of tiny lights glimmered in the dark like fireflies lighting up the night sky. A beam of light shot from the tip of the pyramid into the night sky and Draco wondered if the giant brightly lit sphinx could be seen from space. Maybe one day he would shift into bat form and fly as high as he could go and see how far he could get before he lost sight of the lights, then space could simply swallow him. He was maudlin tonight.

A sigh escaped Draco at the reminder of bats. He walked along the roofline of the Aphelion and practically kicked the tiny creatures out of his path as he went. It was a good thing he had brought his fly swatter for the trip. Draco kicked and then swatted like a master. Bats flew in the air, then moaned as they were smacked aside by his plastic weapon. Draco rolled his eyes. Every night, it was the same bullshit. Being one of the oldest of the vampire race came with too much allure. The younger generations constantly buzzed around him, looking for his attention. They wanted his experience. Obviously, old age came with tons of sexual expertise, but it also came with cynicism and a bad temper. He no longer had the patience for these annoying party-going fools. They were all the same. They wanted blood and sex. All Draco wanted was a quiet night of staring at the stars while dreaming of the sun. Instead, he got to spank ridiculous bats with too hairy of asses.

Draco paused with his fly swatter held high as a diaper-wearing bat zipped past his face. "Are you wearing a nappy?"

The tiny bat hovered inches from Draco's face. He spoke around his thumb. "Yep."

"Why?" Before the bat answered, Draco made a dismissive gesture with his fly swatter. "Never mind. I don't want to know." The bat easily dodged him and latched onto his shoulder. "Where are we going?"

Draco blew out a sigh. "I'm going to work. You're going away."

"Why do you have to work? Aren't you really old? Shouldn't you be retired by now? Shouldn't you have lots of money stashed away somewhere? Can't you just make people give you their money? I don't understand. Every old person I know has lots of money and you have to be way older than them."

Draco pinched the spot between his eyes. "Go away." He swatted his shoulder. The bat disappeared, causing Draco to hit himself. His annoying new accessory reappeared on the opposite shoulder. "I'm Tate. Do you have any choccy milk? I'm thirsty. I've been thirsty a really long time now."

"Do I have any—sweet goddess, what's wrong with you?"

Tate laughed. "I'm not a goddess. Goddesses are girls. I'm a Little."

Another tired-sounding sigh burst from Draco before he could call it back. "Look, Tate. I don't know what you've heard about me, but I'm not looking to play games with children. Go back to your maker, get your nappy changed and your choccy milk or whatever, and leave me in peace. I don't know why everyone thinks pestering me is so much fun, but it's fucking hell on my end. Please go away." Draco swatted again, this time hitting himself on the opposite shoulder when Tate disappeared again.

Tate reappeared on his head, staring directly into his eyes. "Why is it hell? All the other bats have disappeared since I claimed you."

"Since you claimed me..." Draco glanced around. Goddamn it. All the other bats were gone.

"Face it. You need a baby bat to give you peace. Plus, I'm cute and cuddly. You want to keep me." Tate said the words slowly, dragging out each one.

He was a bit adorable. Wait. "Are you trying to use mind control on me?"

An adorable giggle escaped the tiny bat.

With a huff, Draco stopped moving and set his hands on his hips. "Enough of this. Let me look at you. Show yourself." He used a stern voice, ensuring he wouldn't be disobeyed.

Tate gracefully flew from his head, transforming into a blond angel before landing five feet away, draped from head to toe in black. He was flawless in every way. Every vampire was, but this was different. It was obvious Tate had been beautiful before he had turned. Soft-looking blond curls begged to be touched. Light green eyes watched and waited for his approval. He was slight in stature, but he reminded Draco of a ballet dancer he had once known. Small yet powerful. Beautiful.

"I suppose you are keeping away the pests. You can be my assistant tonight, but only for one night, understood?"

Tate bounced on his toes and clapped. "Yay. I'm so excited. You won't regret it."

Draco hid a smile. They would see. He didn't truly care either way. Draco had lived too long to put too much stock into one night no matter which way it went, but this seemed important to Tate. He could spare one evening to learn why. Then tomorrow, Tate would be on his way back to his master and out of Draco's hair. Draco's peace undisturbed... the way it always was and always would be. That was that. Not to mention, one bat beat a thousand any day of the week. Draco would take his breaks where he got them.

To say Tate was disappointed would be a bit of an understatement. When Draco had said assistant, he had thought he would actually be assisting. Instead, Draco had secured him a front-row seat to the show. He supposed things could be worse. Draco could have kicked him to the curb. That hadn't happened yet. Tate just had to make sure he didn't let Draco out of his sight for too long. Not to mention, it was probably for the best Tate wasn't on stage. He didn't feel so good. The stories about being a vampire—so far—had been total bullshit, as far as Tate could tell. Not that he had been a vampire for very long. Two days, actually. It kind of sucked. Everything ached. He was starving, tired, and sick to his stomach. Everything stank and was way too loud, making his head pound. Truth be told, he didn't want to do this forever. Tate really needed this show to be over so Draco could either help him or put him out of his misery. At this point, Tate wasn't sure he cared which.

The magic show was okay. It was probably amazing to the humans. Tricks became pretty bland once a person learned real magic existed. Draco's showmanship wasn't what kept Tate's gaze glued to the stage, though. While the audience clapped for disappearing and multiplying cards, Tate applauded Draco's beauty, because goddamn. Every rumor he had heard from the bats along the way was true. His eyes were black. Tate felt like he wanted to fall into them each time Draco focused on him. Light reflected from his dark hair, reminding Tate of a raven's wings. Tate had never wanted to touch anyone so badly in his life. He sat on the edge of his seat, consumed by lust. Staring at Draco made Tate forget how bad he felt. No one had made his body hum like this in his entire life, and no one understood. Tate was a Little. That wasn't a self-appointed title. Fundamentally, to his core, Tate needed someone to take care of him. He wasn't strong where it counted. Tate's throat swelled at the idea of an eternity with no daddy to care for him. Before two nights ago, he had already been barely getting by, but at least life hadn't been endless. Now, things were surreal and out of his control. He could suddenly do things, unbelievable things, and he felt helpless in a way he couldn't describe. There was nowhere to go for comfort. The bats had whispered one name: Draco Cossus. Now, as Tate stared at him, he knew a level of desperation he had never felt before in his life.

"I need a volunteer."

"Raise your hand."

Tate heard the voice caress his brain. That had only happened to him once before, right before he had been bitten. This time, he knew it was Draco without having to look. He felt him in every fiber of his being—like Draco lived under his skin. He raised his hand.

"Good boy."

Jesus. He was hard as a rock. He loved praise.

Draco's dark gaze scanned the crowd before landing on Tate. He pointed at him. "You. Join me on stage."

As Tate stood, the crowd clapped, and Tate ensured his shirt hid his erection. He held Draco's stare every step of the way. Tate didn't hide his desire from Draco. Draco's lips parted. Tate fought the urge to run into his arms.

"Turn into a bat."

"What? Are you serious? In front of all these people?"

"Yes. Right now. Turn into a bat and fly into my hat."

Tate's lust disappeared. Panic struck. He had never transformed in public before. In fact, he only had the barest under-standing of how he turned into a bat to begin with, but he did as told. The crowd gasped as Tate went from man to tiny bat. He flew through the air, racing to-ward the top hat on the table at Draco's hip.

"Oh, dear. It looks like I might need a dif-ferent volunteer. This one's gone batty."

The crowd laughed as Tate dropped in-side the hat. There was already a bunny inside.

"Oh, my God. A bun bun. I want to smush her adorable face." Tate clung to the bunny's fur. It didn't protest. Tate listened to its steady breathing and heartbeat. *"So sweet."*

"She likes you."

"What's her name?"

"Annabelle."

"Love her."

Tate swore he felt Draco smile inside his mind while he cuddled with the bunny. It had been an amazing night. One Tate didn't want to end, but nothing ever lasted forever. In no time, the show ended. Tate expected Draco to tell him to hit the road. When the curtain dropped and the coast cleared, Tate turned back into a man. This time, he magicked his favorite footed kitty pajamas to cover him. He held Annabelle and watched Draco gather his things. Exhaustion still weighed heavily on his shoulders, but he refused to show it.

"That was amazing. Everyone loved you."

Draco shrugged. "It's a fun way to pass the time. Life gets a bit tedious after a while."

"If you don't mind me asking, how old are you, exactly?"

"I was born the year of our Lord three seventy-three."

"Whoa."

Draco didn't look up from his task, but Tate didn't miss the small smile that touched his lips.

"What did you do back then?"

"I was a soldier for Rome."

Draco eyed him for a moment. He didn't mention Tate's pajamas, which Tate appreciated more than he could say. "Fashion has changed many times over the past sixteen hundred years. I assure you; I rarely consider what anyone is wearing."

Tate blinked. "Can you hear my thoughts?"

"I can hear everyone's thoughts. It's quite annoying sometimes. That's why I prefer the peace no one allows me."

Oh. Now Tate felt guilty.

"Don't. As you pointed out, all the others disappeared once you captured my attention and you're rather different from everyone else."

Tate kept his gaze locked on the calico bunny in his arms and fought a wince. He was more than aware he was an oddity. Everyone had made sure he knew exactly how much he didn't fit in his entire life. Now he would be a square peg in a round world for eternity. It sucked.

"The sun will be up soon. Where are you staying?"

Tate shrugged. He hadn't thought about it.

"Come. You'll stay with me."

With his head down, Tate followed Draco through the back hallways of the hotel to an elevator that needed a key. Draco pulled one from his pocket and let them inside. They went down. The doors opened inside a windowless hotel room. Tate didn't imagine they were underground since it was Vegas. More likely, they were in a concrete bottom corner of the building, protected from the sunlight.

While Draco put his things away, Tate headed for an open playpen area that was obviously Annabelle's home. She jumped into the pen and headed straight for her food bowl the instant he was within leaping distance. He watched her for a moment before wandering around the room and inspecting the place. It was nice, if not impersonal. At Draco's age, Tate would have thought he would have accumulated a ton of clutter. It was like a downstairs penthouse—like Draco had carved out a corner of the building just for himself. His eyes felt heavy. Tate spotted a bed with a black silk comforter. He didn't ask permission before crawling onto the mattress and curling onto his side. Exhaustion weighed too heavily on him for Tate to fight. It had been a long two days. He had nothing left to give.

"Sweet sleep, kitty."

A smile touched Tate's lips as the words caressed his mind. For the first time in memory, Tate felt like he might survive this life, which was only funny since he was technically dead. Life was strange sometimes. He just wished sometimes his wasn't strange all the time.

CHAPTER THREE

TATE WOKE UP ALONE and confused. That happened each day since he—technically—died. Everything in existence was so much louder than it had been when he was mortal. It took much longer than he liked for his senses to stop feeling assaulted. He heard Annabelle chomping on pellets in her cage. The blood pumping through her tiny veins. Electricity hummed through the walls. Draco wasn't there. Tate shot from the bed.

He forced himself not to panic. Tate was still inside Draco's room. He took a breath. Heartbeats bombarded him from every direction, making him want to cower and cover his ears. Then he finally heard it—one heartbeat, half the rate of the rest. Tate took another steadying breath and followed. He spotted Draco's fly swatter on the oak coffee table as he passed. Tate grabbed it on the way to the elevator. He didn't bother changing clothes. Tate didn't want to lose focus and lose Draco. He knew where he was. Draco was on the roof where Tate had met him the night before, but he could easily get away before Tate made the trip upstairs. Thankfully, the elevator went all the way to the roof, so Tate didn't pass any mortals. He was too hungry. Tate didn't know if he could control himself. It felt like it had been ages since he had anything to eat. The thought of human food made his stomach heave.

Bats scattered when Tate stepped off the elevator and onto the roof. His gaze automatically found Draco without having to hunt. Draco barely spared him a glance as Tate moved to sit next to him. The Vegas skyline was beautiful from here. Tate understood why Draco sought solace in this spot.

He passed Draco the fly swatter. "You forgot your beating stick."

A sexy chuckle rumbled from the back of Draco's throat. "I knew you would join me soon enough and the weaklings would flee."

Tate twisted his fingers. He was the weakest link, if he was being honest. Tate didn't know why the other bats scattered when he came around. He was no threat.

"You're starving. When did you last feed?"

Tate shrugged. He scratched the bridge of his nose and tried to block his thoughts. So much humiliation had driven him to find Draco. He didn't know where to start in explaining why he had sought the older vampire's help.

Draco bit his wrist and held it out to Tate. "Drink. My blood is strong. It will hold you much longer than any mortal's will."

Tate couldn't say no. He was too hungry. Too desperate. His lips wrapped around the wound before he had time to think. The hood of his pajamas fell forward, hiding his face and sparing his pride. Tate had been rejected by his maker. Left to die. It didn't happen often, or so he had been told by the bats he had followed to Vegas. Vampires rarely turned a human unless they wanted to keep the person for eternity. Tate's turning had been a cruel joke. He had been tricked into vampirism and then abandoned. Everything he knew how to do as a vampire, he had learned on accident. He had been desperate to find Draco once he learned of his existence, so he had turned into a bat without really trying so he could fly here. Tate had seen some pajamas he had really wanted along the way, so he made them with his mind. When he felt the sun coming, he followed the other bats inside caves and hid until darkness freed him again. Tate had survived, but barely. He didn't want to be strong. Tate wanted to go back to being the Little he had once been before his life had been stolen from him. Things hadn't been great before his turning, but at least he had felt like his life belonged to him. Everything felt out of his control now. Tate didn't know to feed himself as a vampire. He had never bitten anyone. He didn't know how to do anything. Likely, he would be dead within a week.

Draco pushed Tate's hood aside and stroked his hair. "Tell me how you ended up like this."

Tate licked Draco's wrist a final time, and the wound healed. He felt better than he had in ages, but he still fought tears. Tate hated how exposed he felt. "I'm sure you can look into my mind and see whatever you want."

"I'd rather hear it from you."

Draco looked kind at that moment. The dark eyes that had stared at him with such lust the night before now held a gentleness he needed more than words could say. Tate heard himself speak without thinking. "I was at a fetish club in New Orleans." A sad smile pulled at Tate's lips. He had never known how to explain himself to other people. To people who weren't like him. "At first, I thought it was just a game. Everything there is supposed to be a game." Tate couldn't stop wringing his hands. It was out of his control. He hated thinking about that night. "I just wanted a daddy. That's the only reason I was there. But he hurt me, and I was scared. Then it turned out he only bit me as a joke. His sister thought it would be funny for him to turn a little pervert like me." Tate used air quotes, trying to hide how much those words had hurt. They still hurt. He had been different his whole life. But inside a fetish club, he was supposed to be safe. He was supposed to fit in, but Tate never fit in anywhere, and now he was an even bigger oddity than ever before. Tate fought the urge to rub his chest. He couldn't meet Draco's stare any longer. A bitter smile touched his lips. "Maybe a few hundred years will cure me of all my strange human desires."

"I was turned when I was twenty-six. It has been over sixteen hundred years since I've last seen the sun."

The longing in Draco's voice had Tate turning his head and meeting Draco's stare again. What he saw in Draco's eyes made it impossible for Tate to look away. "Why do you think I sit out here every night despite the flying horde of horny imbeciles?" Draco didn't wait for Tate to guess. "It's because I still crave the sensation of the sun on my skin. The bright Vegas lights are as close as I'll ever get. So, no. I don't believe you ever grow out of human desires." The tips of Draco's fangs showed as he made the claim, making butterflies stir in Tate's stomach at the sight. "You may stay with me. I will teach you to feed. You can teach me what a Little does."

Tate pressed his lips together to keep from crying out in his excitement... or just crying. He forced his voice to remain steady. "Are you sure you won't be ashamed of me? Basically, I just like to be treated like a spoiled child." His gaze dropped to those goddamn sexy fangs again without permission from his brain. "I still like to get fucked, though."

A wicked smile stretched Draco's lips. He laughed. The sound had chill bumps rising on Tate's skin. He genuinely felt good in Draco's company.

Draco stood and held his hand out to Tate. As he did, his outfit changed, becoming a tuxedo and top hat. "Let's go, beautiful. You have no fear I'll be ashamed."

Tate accepted his outstretched hand. "Where are we going?"

"I'm the great Draco Cossus. Every night in Vegas is an adventure. You can be my white rabbit." He snapped the fingers of his free hand and Tate's one-piece pajamas became a fuzzy white rabbit costume. Draco lifted Tate from his feet. "Piggyback ride?"

Tate squealed and scrambled to Draco's back. He didn't know how long Draco would allow this before he got bored, but Tate would take whatever he could get. As long as he wasn't alone, Tate could handle anything else. After dying, everything else looked like a breeze.

First things first, Tate needed a night to just have fun. So far, he had only seen the downside of vampirism. It had its upsides too—like getting whatever they wanted. Draco headed for the nightclub inside the hotel. No one stopped them. Everyone knew Draco and wouldn't question any guest he had in tow. Tate clung to his back like a monkey, feeling lighter than a feather. His presence was like feeling the sunshine on his face for the first time in nearly two thousand years. Draco didn't know how else to describe it. Tate had taken Draco's blood and now he couldn't hide anything from Draco. His rainbows and lollipop brain bombarded Draco's darkness. Tate needed a protector. It filled Draco with seething rage to think of the cruel trick that had been played on Tate. Vampirism wasn't a game. It was eternity. Without a keeper, someone like Tate wouldn't survive.

Sultry music filled the air. Draco flipped Tate over his shoulder. Tate's squeals of delight had a smile tugging at his lips as he spun Tate onto the dance floor. The way Tate stayed balanced on the toes of Draco's shoes made him laugh with delight. He couldn't explain his mood. Draco wasn't normally like this. He was the brooding type when he wasn't on stage. Perhaps this was a new version of showmanship for him. He paraded a new prize to the crowd.

Draco lifted Tate so he could touch his lips to Tate's ear without straining his back. "It's time to choose our prey." He spun Tate in his arms and moved with the music while holding Tate against his chest. Draco didn't miss the way Tate's breathing changed. He forced himself to focus on the crowd instead of the perfect body in his arms. A middle-aged man sat alone near the dance floor, nursing a drink. It was obvious he wanted to join the fun, but he wasn't brave enough to ask anyone to dance.

"*Look at me.*" Draco sent the silent command across the room.

The man's head turned their way. He focused on Draco and Tate dancing. Draco held the man's stare as he kissed Tate's ear, tempting the stranger on to the dance floor.

"Join us."

The man stood. His business suit was a bit disheveled, as if he had spent the day working or traveling. Draco didn't care enough to search his thoughts to find out. He only wanted the mortal's blood.

He moved to stand toe to toe with them. His gaze moved between Draco and Tate. "Hi. I'm Mike."

Tate giggled.

Mike smiled.

Draco smirked. "Hi, Mike. You should join us."

That was all it took to draw Mike into their dance. Draco led Tate's hands to Mike's chest. He kept Mike hypnotized while Tate unwound Mike's tie and unbuttoned his shirt.

"Listen for his heartbeat."

Tate's mouth touched Mike's chest.

Draco fought an unexpected hint of jealousy. This was survival. Tate had to learn how to properly feed. When Tate had drunk his blood earlier, Draco had seen his memories. Tate had a friend who worked at a blood bank. The man had given Tate a few bags of blood to sustain him until Tate could find Draco for help. Tate was damn lucky not to be dead. Bagged blood was one step away from being toxic to them. But Tate hadn't known how to feed, and he hadn't wanted to hurt anyone. Draco would help him.

Tate kissed a path to Mike's neck. Mike moaned and swayed closer. Their dance turned more intimate by the second.

Draco used his size to keep Tate hidden between them.

"Follow your instincts."

Tate bit.

Mike gasped.

Tate almost pulled away, but Draco stopped him.

"That was a gasp of pleasure, sweet kitty. Keep going. You'll know when to stop."

Draco listened for the telltale change in heart rhythm. Tate dutifully retracted his fangs and licked the wound closed.

"It was nice meeting you, Mike. You're exhausted. You should go to bed."

Mike nodded. "I'm exhausted. It was nice meeting you. I think I'll head to bed."

As Mike walked away, Tate spun. "I did it." The happiness and excitement in Tate's eyes were something Draco hadn't experienced himself in more years than he recalled. "You did. I never doubted you. Now it's your turn. You must teach me one thing."

Tate's expression changed, turning sweet. He climbed Draco's body until Draco held him on his hip. His lips whisked Draco's cheek. "Thank you, Daddy. Can you show me how to suck something else now?" Tate popped his thumb in his mouth, looking innocent, as if he hadn't weakened Draco's knees. His sexy green eyes stayed locked on Draco with zero shame.

Draco gently pushed Tate's hand aside. He cupped Tate's cheek. Tate's eyes closed, and he nuzzled Draco's hand, making his chest tighten with an emotion he hadn't felt in centuries. "That's a shame." The whispered words fell from Draco's lips without thought. Tate's eyes opened. With his vampire sense, he wouldn't have missed a word. His innocent green gaze focused on Draco. Confusion etched his features. "What's a shame?"

"I've just realized how much it'll hurt when you leave."

The line between Tate's eyebrows deepened. "Maybe I won't." He sounded so adorably defiant. Draco couldn't help but smile.

"Ah, sweet kitty, do you have any idea how many freshly turned vampires have found me over the years and promised themselves to me for eternity? If I had a stone for every one of them,

I could build a pyramid that would rival the Giza."

"This is the first time you've met anyone like me."

There was such sweet power in Tate. Draco already knew how they would end. Tate would grow stronger and more restless. He would tire of the quiet life Draco lived. Eventually, he would want all the adventure Draco had already experienced. That was fair. Draco couldn't deny him that, but damn. He already knew this one would hurt a little more than the rest. Tate was special. He made Draco smile again. This was a dangerous game. Draco had no plans to stop. That didn't mean he was blind or dumb. He would lose the way he always did in the end, but what a ride it would be until then.

For Tate, there had always been a strange power in being a Little. His ability to regress into innocence spoke to certain men and made him feel strong when he had always been weak. There was also a scary power in being the center of Draco's attention. Tate heard what Draco said about the many newly turned vampires that had come before him. He saw the pain in Draco's eyes. But Tate knew himself and always had. He was a Little for a reason. Tate longed to find one man who he could love and cherish forever. He wanted to be one man's baby for eternity. Tate never wanted life to be a game. He didn't know how to make Draco see that truth other than to never leave.

"Do you plan to kiss me in front of all these people, or are you waiting until you have me alone?"

Draco's smirk left him enchanted. "You tell me. Reach into my mind and take what you want."

Although Tate realized this was meant to be another lesson on learning about his powers, his patience was gone. He pressed his lips against Draco's. Tate's skin tingled, like millions of ants crawled over him. The air shifted, making it harder to breathe. His back hit a soft surface and Draco's body came down on top of his. His mind registered they had somehow shifted through time and space and landed safely in Draco's bed, but nothing mattered except Draco's mouth opening over his. He sucked Tate's bottom lip. Draco barely teased him, nibbling. Tate couldn't focus on anything else. The teeth on the zipper of his pajamas released one at a time as Draco slowly unzipped the outfit. Tate panted. He had never felt more useless. Their tongues hadn't even met yet and Tate was a fucking mess. Then Draco's tongue stroked his, and the world stopped turning. Tate kept a death grip on Draco's shirt, trying not to explode into a million stars. He hadn't known a person could want anything as badly as he wanted Draco.

There was a newly unleashed predator inside him, making Tate stronger than he had ever been, but that was not who he was on a visceral level. He needed to be the weaker one. Tate craved what he had never been given: love and care.

Draco's touch stayed soft. He was so gentle with Tate. It nearly brought tears to Tate's eyes. His short twenty-two years on earth had been so hard. He so desperately wanted to be special to someone. His parents had been young teens when Tate had been born, and neither had wanted him. But they had been too scared of their parents to give Tate up for adoption, so Tate had been passed from house to unwelcoming house as a kid. He had found being quiet, making himself small, and staying hidden was the key to survival into adulthood. His short foray into being grown hadn't been much better. He had made a friend while selling plasma to survive. Cosmos had introduced him to fetish clubs. That was where he had found himself, but still no softness or caring had found him. No love. Damned if Draco's touch didn't trick his brain now. He couldn't help but wonder if this was what love felt like.

"Love is much better. It takes time. I'm cherishing you for the gift you are."

Heat exploded through Tate's face. "Please stop reading my mind." Even Tate heard the horror in his voice.

Draco sat back on his heels. In one smooth motion, he peeled off his jacket before tossing it aside. Then his shirt magically disappeared. Tate forgot to be embarrassed. He saw the Roman soldier then. Tate's hands moved to Draco's belt. They shook. Draco watched him like he mattered.

"Touch me."

The pleading in Draco's voice nearly broke him. He sounded every bit as desperate as Tate felt. Even though Tate knew it couldn't possibly be true, he liked to think Draco might need him every bit as much as Tate had to have him. Maybe his existence wasn't pointless after all.

When he finally brushed his fingertips down Draco's stomach and curled his fingers around his belt, Draco drew a ragged breath like he had been waiting all night for Tate's touch. Chill bumps rose on Tate's skin at the sound. He pulled open Draco's belt and unbuttoned his pants. Tate licked his lips as he slid down Draco's zipper. He swore he could already taste Draco's cock on his tongue.

"Goddamn. You're killing me."

Tate beat back an evil smile at Draco's confession as he set Draco's erection free. Then his breath left him. Draco leaked for him. Tate swirled his fingertip through the pre-cum, wetting Draco's crown.

"May I please put it in my mouth?"

A whimper came from the back of Draco's throat as his clothes vanished and he crawled up Tate's body, leading his dick to Tate's lips. Tate obediently opened. A relieved sigh left him as Draco's cock scraped his tongue. He sucked, soothing himself. The past few days had been so stressful, with no relief. He couldn't recall the last time anything pacified him this much.

Tate clutched Draco's ass and squeezed, holding on while he sucked, savoring the peace that settled over him. Then Draco's pleasure slammed into his mind. It was as if his brain finally relaxed enough to let Draco in and fuck. Tate had his hand inside his fire truck underwear before he could stop himself. He stroked as he let Draco fuck his throat. Everything felt too good. He swore he felt everything he did to Draco. It was like he sucked his own dick. Tate put everything into the act while Draco rode his face.

"That's it, lovely. I know you feel this. See how good you are. You're a good boy. You can take the whole thing. Fuck. That feels good."

Tate breathed through his nose. With his eyes closed, he stayed focused on the building pressure. He projected the pleasure of his palm to Draco while absorbing the ecstasy of his mouth. The moment was unlike anything he had ever experienced. Tate didn't know how things would end, but he had a bad feeling he would never be the same once he came. He pumped faster and sucked harder. A moment before he thought he would blow, Draco flipped, turning around. His cock was immediately back in Tate's mouth before Tate knew what happened. His clothes vanished. He expected Draco would return the favor. Instead, Draco's fangs sank into his femoral artery. A scream might have ripped from him if cum hadn't filled his mouth. Tate swallowed. The world became like a dream. All he knew was pleasure and uncontrollable shaking. His body no longer belonged to him. Cum filled the space between them and Tate couldn't direct where it went. All he could do was drink Draco's cum and ride out the waves of nonstop pleasure. He had never had an orgasm like this one. In fact, this one made him feel like he had never had an orgasm before. It seemed to go on forever while Tate was useless to do anything but accept it. Then Draco held him and kissed him. He was clean, warm, and cuddled with no memory of how he went from covered in cum to tucked into bed. Life had a surreal edge that made everything feel like a dream.

"Whoa."

A sexy-sounding chuckle rumbled from Draco at Tate's obvious shock.

Tate blinked at the ceiling, trying to decipher what just happened and if he would ever be the same. "Draco?" Tate didn't know why he whispered.

"Hmm?"

"Can I call you daddy?" He realized he should have asked that earlier, before calling Draco daddy the first time. Communication and consent were important.

"I'd like that."

The smile in Draco's voice warmed Tate's heart. He felt more powerful and happier in that moment than he had in his entire life. For the first time, he saw a future for himself where he built a good life with a good man. He knew Draco didn't see that life yet, but Tate would show him. He was a good boy. Tate could make him happy. They would have a great life together. He would make Draco see.

CHAPTER FOUR

THE SUN STOLE TATE from him longer than Draco liked. When it fell and the moon rose, Draco ran a bubble bath for his kitty bat. He hated to leave him alone for any length of time, but they needed to feed. Draco would hunt for them both. He didn't go far. Draco cornered the closest member of the hotel's hospitality staff and drank for two. The woman would be woozy for about two hours, but he saw in her mind she wanted to leave for the day anyhow. This would give her the excuse she needed to go home early.

The moment he could, Draco zipped back to Tate. It was a bit disconcerting how easily Tate had gotten under his skin. In his defense, Draco had been alone for a long time. But it was more than that. Tate hadn't been meant for this life. He shouldn't have been chosen for this struggle. Vampirism was a long, hard, and lonely path. Eternity wasn't for the weak. Tate was a soft soul. He was too pure for what had been thrust upon him. A cruel, evil joke had been played on him. Draco would not stand by and let that misdeed pass. He couldn't pretend he didn't know this injustice had been done.

For much longer than necessary, Draco stood inside the bathroom doorway and watched Tate play. He was a fresh light in a dark world, easing Draco's tired soul. "Splashy. Splashy. Stomp. Stomp."

Tate turned into a little bat and then a bigger bat, splashing and swirling in the tub, sending bubbles flying in every direction like a bat tornado. His voice changed from light to deep depending on his size, making Draco's smile grow.

"Are you having fun?"

Tate turned human and grabbed his head, as if the room spun. "Whoa. I went too fast."

There were bubbles on his head and the tip of his nose. Draco couldn't stop smiling. With a flick of his wrist, his clothes melted away and Draco stepped into the tub with Tate.

Tate's childlike demeanor immediately vanished as he straddled Draco's hips and scooted closer until their cocks bumped. "Hello, Daddy. Did you miss me?"

"Immensely."

A shy smile touched Tate's lips. "Why did you want to hunt without me?"

"Reach into my mind and see for yourself." Tate needed to learn this skill. Draco was much older and a lot more powerful. He had to open his mind for Tate, but it was important for Tate to learn how to survive. Draco felt Tate's mind tentatively touch his before quickly retreating again. It must have been enough.

Tate's expression moved through a series of emotions before landing on shocked. "You don't want me to bite anyone else."

Draco shook his head. "I know it's ridiculous. I know you'll eventually move on, but as long as you're here, I enjoy feeding you. It's my job to take care of you."

Tate bit his bottom lip, looking sweet and sexy. "Oh. Well, what can I do for you, then? You know, to return the favor."

Stay.

Draco didn't mean to think the plea quite so loudly. He wouldn't beg, but nor would he lie to himself. Tate's presence in his life had renewed his spirit. He didn't want Tate to leave.

Tate scooted even closer. His gaze dropped to Draco's mouth. Water rolled down his face, doing nothing to soften his heated expression. "I already intended to stay. What can I do besides that? Do you like to get bit? Like the way you bit me."

Draco fought to control his breathing. He was already hard as a rock. Tate was a wonderful mixture of innocent and naughty. It was obvious he knew how to play men and Draco was here for it. "You'll have to bite me no matter what since you need to feed, but yes. Wherever you choose to bite me, I'll like it as much as you did."

Tate licked his lips, looking nervous. "What'll happen if you're inside me when I bite you?"

Fuck. He was such a tease. Draco made a subtle motion and the water drained from the tub. He snapped his fingers and lube appeared in his hand. "You should find out, don't you think?"

Tate took the lube from him. He held Draco's stare as he coated Draco's cock. Tate's touch felt amazing. It was soft and loving—like reverence. Tate positioned himself over Draco's erection. Draco let him have complete control. He enjoyed allowing Tate to use him like a toy.

Tate laughed. "I like that. You're a bath toy."

A smile snapped to Draco's lips. Tate had read his mind. Whether he realized it or not remained to be seen, but he had done so. Draco was proud of him.

With his head thrown back, eyes squeezed shut, and a look of pure ecstasy etched on his face, Tate impaled himself with Draco's cock. A shaky-sounding breath escaped him. "I enjoy making you proud."

Draco's insides twisted with pleasure. Tate's expression alone was enough to send him over the edge, but adding that with his excruciatingly tight little asshole and Draco didn't know how long he would last.

Tate's eyes opened.

Their gazes collided.

Draco nearly came. He had never seen a purer lust. "You look more turned on than anyone I've ever seen."

"I'm not used to getting what I want."

Draco would give him the world. Then Tate would realize nothing was beyond his grasp any longer and he would leave. A wave of pain washed over Draco at the thought.

"You're hurting."

Draco cupped Tate's face. "I'm used to losing things."

Tate clutched Draco's shoulders and leaned closer, lowering his head. His lips touched Draco's pulse point beneath his ear. "I'm very different from everyone else you've ever met." Tate's fangs sank into Draco's skin, making him see stars. For the first time in his life, he believed in something bigger than himself. Even if that faith only lasted for a few moments, while Tate drank from him and fucked him at the same time, Draco believed with his entire chest that Tate would stay, and they would be happy. For a moment, everything looked beautiful. Draco had never wanted to keep something so badly in his entire life. He would die for it.

Tate had never felt so full. His heart, head, and body were bursting with more than he could handle. He honestly hadn't known what he would find here in Vegas. It wasn't this. There was no way he could have foreseen this amazing man. Tate would die if he lost him, and they had just met. He forced himself to retract his fangs and lick the wound closed. The sounds Draco made while Tate bounced on his dick made him feel powerful. He was in control. A little too powerful. Too much in control.

His teeth chattered. The temperature dropped in the room. Tate's skin chilled. Vulnerability set in. No one watched his back. He couldn't protect Draco if anyone burst into the bathroom. Tate fought the urge to check over his shoulder. He needed to know he was safe.

Draco shot from the tub, clutching Tate to his chest. Tate found his back braced against the nearest wall. Draco held his stare as he used Tate's body. He was so fucking strong. It took Tate's breath. All Tate could do was hang on while Draco fucked him. Draco felt amazing inside Tate, hitting at the perfect angle. Tate's dick bounced in the air as Draco pounded his ass. The sound of skin slapping against skin at an unnatural speed filled the air. Still, they never looked away from each other. Tate forgot to be scared.

"You will come for me, then you'll help me do my magic show. Afterward, you'll tell me who hurt you and makes you watch your back."

Draco's demand almost took Tate out of the mood, except Draco still controlled his body. There was no denying the things he did. "Make me come."

An evil-sounding chuckle rumbled from Draco at Tate's taunt. Draco swapped his hold, easily keeping Tate against the wall with one arm while he gripped Tate's cock with his free hand. In a motion too fast to see with the human eye, he speed-jacked Tate's dick.

A loud cry ripped from Tate's throat as an orgasm tore from him without warning. Another followed before he had a chance to recover from the first. Cum coated his skin. His body shook. He couldn't think. Draco didn't stop until Tate came a third time and Tate was ready to cry for real. It was almost painful to come so fast, so close together. It was unnerving. Then he felt Draco's orgasm build. He couldn't focus on anything else. The connection of their minds was such a beautiful thing. It was breathtaking. He couldn't look away as

Draco came. Tate lost his breath. He was so gorgeous. Tate had never seen anyone more lovely.

Even as Draco pulled out and cleaned Tate's body, Tate watched him in awe. He was like the eighth wonder of the world. Draco kept Tate mystified.

"Are you ready to become a full-time magician's assistant?" Draco asked unexpectedly.

A tired-sounding laugh burst from Tate. Here he was, thinking about how beautiful and amazing Draco was, and Draco was planning Tate's future employment. "This hotel really lets you do whatever you want, don't they?"

"Of course they do," Draco said with a laugh. "I own it."

Tate blinked. "You own it?"

A dark, laughing gaze met his stare. "Of course. What do you think I've been doing all these years in Vegas? This is my hotel. I built it specifically for my needs and entertainment. Well, our needs now."

A laugh burst from Tate. Despite his newfound ability to read minds, Draco still surprised him. "I can't wait to spend eternity with you."

Draco's smile faltered. He wanted to believe. Tate felt that, but he still wasn't quite there yet. He would be. Draco would see.

"Tell me what an assistant does," Tate said, rather than trying to convince him. He had forever to make Draco believe he wasn't going anywhere. There was no need to rush. They may as well go to work. He still had a lot to learn about being a vampire. They had until the end of time to work on their relationship. Tate couldn't wait to get started.

CHAPTER FIVE

CRADLED IN A TOP hat—in bat form—Tate wore a diaper, a white rabbit onesie, and sucked a binkie. He stared up at Draco with his heart in his eyes. Draco wowed the crowd the way he did every night. Eight months was a drop in a barrel of time for Draco, Tate was sure. But for Tate, the past eight months with Draco had been the best of his life. Eight months was the longest anyone had been willing to keep him while actually wanting to do so. He was in love. Tate knew without a doubt he would die without Draco at his side. That had nothing to do with Draco feeding and bathing him. Love was its own necessity. A person could choose to curl up and starve. Tate couldn't choose a life without Draco. Insanity waited on the other side of that door.

"I shall now pull a rabbit out of my hat. I know it's an old trick, but..." Draco reached inside the hat. Tate did his bit by slowly turning human as Draco tried pulling him out of the top hat by the rabbit ears of his costume.

"Damn. I must have brought the wrong hat."

The crowd laughed as Draco stuffed Tate back inside the hat and Tate turned back into a tiny bat. He snuggled back down to wait for the end of Draco's show.

A burning tingle crawled over Tate's skin—like fire ants stinging him. *"I feel something yucky."*

"I feel it too."

Tate reached out with his senses. It was like someone sat in the crowd who was vampire, yet they weren't, or maybe they were blocking him. Tate couldn't tell. He couldn't figure it out, but their intentions didn't feel pure. They wanted something. Dark desire pulsed from them. It wasn't lust. They needed... something. Tate nearly growled in his frustration at trying to work it out. He had felt nothing like it before. The worst part was the way Draco's mind had gone quiet to him, as if there was something he hid from Tate.

Draco finished his show without missing a beat. No one who watched would know anything was amiss by looking at him. As the curtain fell, Tate expected Draco would quickly sweep them away, fleeing from the dark energy that pulsed from every direction. Instead, Draco lingered. Even though Tate wanted to scream, he didn't make a sound. Draco might have looked as if he didn't pay attention to his surroundings, but Tate felt the way he watched and waited.

"Ollie and Olivia. It's been years."

Tate started when Draco spoke. He didn't look away from staring inside his hat, which doubled Tate's confusion.

"It has been."

The man's voice carried from a distance but moved closer, making Tate realize Draco spoke to someone he hadn't felt approaching.

"You know we don't make it out this way often. The time difference and all." This time, it was a woman's voice.

The closer they came, the colder Tate's skin turned. His teeth chattered. He locked his jaw around his pacifier against the sensation.

"Of course." Their gazes met. "*Don't move or make a sound.*"

Tate didn't need to be told. He didn't like the way he felt.

"A rumor recently reached our ears that you have something that belongs to us."

Draco covered Tate with a handker-chief. "I know that can't be true since I haven't seen either of you in decades."

"You know that's not what I mean, so don't play coy."

Tate's blood ran cold at the familiar hiss of the stranger's voice. He realized it wasn't a stranger at all. Tate knew that voice. He had felt it against his skin. It hit him why he felt so uneasy and why he couldn't read the pair. One was his maker. Tate's heart sped. His breathing turned rapid. He didn't understand why he couldn't read the female vampire, but he knew Ollie. Tate hadn't known his name. At least, not his real name. Many people went by different names at fetish clubs to protect themselves. Usually, they hoped to shield their jobs or whatever. Tate couldn't even recall what name Ollie had given him that night. Maybe he hadn't given him one at all. All he remembered was the pain and Ollie's laughter. Tate couldn't breathe.

The room spun and Tate found himself sitting in the center of the bed he shared with Draco in human form. He tried reaching out to Draco, but there was nothing but silence. Draco had sent him away and then shut the door between their minds. Tate wanted to scream. He fought the urge to race upstairs to the theater to intervene. Tate hadn't been disconnected from Draco's mind in eight months. The silence was deafening. He had never felt emptier. Instead of acting on his impulses, he sat frozen, wringing his hands. Tate had always been such a useless thing. It was no wonder no one ever wanted to keep him. Draco should have followed the pattern of the rest. Choosing to keep Tate might end up getting him killed.

A tear landed on his wrist. He stared at it in surprise. Tate hadn't even realized he was crying. He was terrified and angry at himself. If his maker was here, claiming

Draco had stolen Tate, would Tate have to leave with him? Tate didn't know the rules. He still didn't completely understand this world. Ollie had shown for a reason. It wasn't for any good one. Of that, Tate was sure. Tate had been so happy here. He already felt his security slipping away. Nothing good ever lasted for him. He wasn't allowed to have peace. Tate should have known he wouldn't be allowed to keep Draco. His life was only pain. Panic had him in its grip and he didn't know how to make it stop. In his heart, Tate already knew he had lost. He didn't know how to change the outcome of the game.

From the first time Draco had looked into Tate's mind and seen who had turned him, he had known this night would come. The twins, Ollie and Olivia, were known for their cruelty. The pair had been turned against their will and worked to make it everyone's problem ever since. They had been whores, working the underbelly of London in the early eighteen hundreds. Twins who would do anything for a price had been a draw for one particularly nasty vampire back in those days. Draco imagined the pair had lived through hell, but that did not give them license to do the same to his angel. Draco wouldn't allow it.

"Why are you really here?" Draco met Ollie's cold ice-blue stare. He was much older and stronger than the twins would ever be. Draco had no clue what they hoped to gain by challenging him.

A cruel smile twisted Ollie's lips. Deep dimples appeared in his cheeks. He cast his dark-haired twin a laughing gaze. Her curls bobbed as they exchanged a look before Ollie met Draco's stare again. "I told you. Rumor has it you have my ward. I want my toy back."

"No." Draco didn't play games. He didn't plan to start tonight.

Olivia laughed. "Such cheek."

Ollie's smile grew. "You don't get a choice here, Draco. You might be ancient, but you don't make the rules. All I have to do is call to him and he'll have no choice but to come… like a well-trained dog. That is how it works. He's mine. I made him. You don't get to say no."

"Yet I did. No."

Ollie's smile fell. His eyes flashed with anger. "And again, you can't tell me no."

"Then call him," Draco taunted. He held Ollie's stare, silently daring him to try. Draco didn't wait to see what Ollie would do before pushing him further. "Do you even feel him here, or are you only going by these supposed rumors? I'm genuinely confused to why you would challenge me like this."

A flicker of uncertainty flashed across Ollie's features. He cast another glance Olivia's way.

An evil smile stretched Draco's lips. He knew Ollie had tried silently calling to

Tate, to no avail. Draco heard him. "It didn't work, did it? Are you asking yourself why? Maybe you should try saying the words out loud. How many vampires have you made in your lifetime, Ollie? Do you truly know the rules?" Draco took a step in Ollie's direction with each question. He didn't wait for Ollie to figure things out for himself. "You see, if you knew anything at all about being a maker, you'd know you could simply snap your fingers and your ward would appear."

Draco snapped his fingers and Tate appeared in his arms. He was openly crying. Draco kept Tate's face turned away from the twins. He would never give them the satisfaction of seeing Tate's tears. Draco swiped Tate's cheek. "It's okay, baby. Daddy will only be a few minutes longer. You don't have to worry while you wait." He waved his hand and sent Tate back to bed before meeting Ollie's surprised stare. "Or you could flick your wrist and send them away."

Rage boiled in Ollie's eyes. "Bring back my minion. He isn't yours. He's mine." Ollie looked one step away from stamping his foot like a child.

"Is he, though?" Even Draco couldn't believe how calm he sounded, considering the rage that filled his entire being. Ollie had really thought he would waltz in and take the other half of Draco's soul and live to tell the tale. It was laughable. Draco kept talking only to stop himself from ripping out Ollie's throat and leaving a mess for his staff. "When you turned Tate, did you even try? Or did you simply smear some blood across his lips and hope it stuck?" Draco clasped his hands behind his back, feigning a relaxed pose he didn't feel. "There's so much more to being a maker than simply draining a human and giving them a hint of your blood. Do you recall your turning? I remember mine. It was several nights of blood and sex and bonding. You're weak. You don't have what it takes to be a maker."

"You—"

Draco shot forward, snagging Ollie's throat, cutting off whatever words he thought to spew. Olivia attacked from the side. Draco held her throat before she made it two steps. The pair tried shifting to bat form, falling right into his trap. Draco dragged the pair through time and space before reappearing on the rooftop. He shoved them inside an iron cage and slammed the door shut before they could shift again.

Draco gripped the bars in his rage even though it burned his skin. He eyed the pair as they flew in circles, singeing their wings on the bars. "One of two things is about to happen. Either another vampire will rescue you before the sun rises in the next few hours, or they won't. Either way, consider yourselves dead, because I'd better never see you again. No one hurts my baby boy and lives to tell about it. Good luck to you both."

Draco made his way back to Tate by taking the long way. He needed a moment to calm down. Rage pulsed through his veins as he rode the elevator to his room. The twins had genuinely thought they would simply walk into his hotel and take away what belonged to him. He was an ancient vampire. His blood was more powerful than most creatures alive today. Part of Draco hoped the pair lived, so they spread the word. He would see anyone dead who ever thought to pull another stunt like this again. The disrespect was unheard of. It wasn't done.

The lift dinged. Draco took a breath to calm himself before stepping into the home he shared with Tate. Eight months might not be much time in comparison to his long life, but it was the start to their journey to eternity. He wouldn't allow the beauty of them to be tainted by any further doubts. Draco found Tate waiting in the center of the bed. His face was splotchy from crying, but no more tears streaked his face. Even though his eyes were red, and his lashes were still wet, it was obvious he had chosen to trust in Draco. He made Draco proud.

"What are we going to do now?"

Draco's eyebrows rose at the question. "What do you mean?"

Tate's bottom lip quivered, making Draco's chest squeeze. "My maker is here to take me away."

A smile touched Draco's lips. He crawled onto the bed and gathered Tate into his arms. "Baby, I'm your maker."

Tate rolled so fast to go nose to nose with Draco he nearly knocked Draco's teeth out. "What are you talking about? I know I'm a little dumb sometimes, but I'm not that stupid. You didn't turn me."

Draco slapped Tate's ass hard enough to make Tate rub the sting. "Don't call yourself dumb or stupid. I won't tolerate that." He held Tate's stare, waiting for a response.

Finally, Tate nodded. "Yes, Daddy."

Appeased, Draco gave him a sharp nod. "When I first met you, I read your thoughts and saw your journey here. I was confused at first because I saw your friend giving you bags of blood to survive after Ollie's half-assed turning. Bagged blood should have killed you. It's basically toxic to vampires, but you survived. Thank the goddesses for your weird friend Cosmos and you following the whisperings of the bats. Otherwise, you never would have found me. I digress, though. By piecing together your memories, I realized Ollie had only given you enough blood to turn you but not enough to actually sustain you. It was barely a drop. When you awoke with fangs, I was truly the first living being you drank from. I'm an ancient. My blood is incredibly powerful. It basically burned away any traces of Ollie's blood in your system. You belong to me. I'm the who kept you alive and who bonded with you. Without me, you would not have survived. That makes me your true maker."

Tate stared at him in silence, blinking for a full minute. His thoughts raced in too many directions for Draco to follow. "Did you know that would happen when you offered me your wrist that first time?" As Tate asked the question, his mind went still. Draco felt how important his answer was to Tate, but it was obvious he didn't want Draco to know how important it was to him.

"Yes. I knew."

Tate's lips parted in surprise. "You chose that, even though you didn't really want me."

"I wanted you."

Even Draco felt the way his fangs grew and brushed his bottom lip at the claim. It was as if his entire body couldn't help but respond to Tate. There was no one more desired.

Tate's gaze dropped to Draco's mouth. He licked his lips as he stared at Draco's mouth. "So, I don't have to live in fear of Ollie any longer?"

"You never did. I was always here to protect you."

Tate wiggled closer. "Are you ready to admit yet that you know I'm not going anywhere?"

"If it pleases you for me to do so, then yes."

Tate's gaze lifted. His eyes glowed a little brighter than usual. He slid the zipper down on his pajamas as he held Draco's stare. "Are you also willing to admit you love me?"

"If it pleases you for me to do so, then yes."

Tate bit his bottom lip, visibly fighting a smile. "What can I do to please you?"

"Admit you love me too."

Unexpectedly, tears filled Tate's eyes. He blinked them away. "I do, Daddy. Don't you feel it?"

Draco rolled, pinning Tate beneath him. Tate's love screamed at him all hours of the day. It was the reason Draco could no longer pretend Tate would one day walk away when he wasn't looking. There was no way he couldn't believe in Tate. Tate's love was the most powerful thing Draco had encountered in all his years of life. He wanted more. Draco was a glutton for the emotions pouring from Tate. They were both so goddamn needy, and it worked. Draco saw their beautiful future, and it was filled with all the happiness. He had never been more thankful for Tate's ability to make a little pest of himself when he wanted. Otherwise, he might not have stood out from the rest, but he had. Thank all the goddesses, because he had found the greatest love of his life in the smallest of bats.

"Do you plan to make love to me now?"

A smile that felt wicked even to Draco pulled at Draco's lips. "Later. Right now, I plan to fuck you. I don't feel like being soft."

"Okay." It was the sweetest acquiescence. Music to Draco's ears. Now he wanted to hear him scream.

CHAPTER SIX

"COMING TO YOU LIVE from Aphelion Hotel, Channel Seven has exclusive access to the ten-year anniversary special of a lifetime. The Great Draco Cossus and his husband Tate celebrate ten years of magic together."

Draco stared at Tate while Tate watched an internet clip of their show from earlier that night. He still couldn't believe ten years had passed. It had come and gone in a blink of an eye. Draco never tired of the tiny bat that had flown into his life. Tate's beauty grew in his eyes each day.

Tate glanced his way. "You look so sexy. I spend most of my night inside your hat, so I miss the way people stare at you with longing."

Draco hated to ignore Tate's compliment, but they needed to talk. "Speaking of everyone looking at me, tonight was likely our last show."

After turning off the tablet, Tate quietly set it aside while avoiding his stare. His gaze scanned the skyline. The Vegas lights made his blond curls shimmer. "I'll admit, I've wondered lately how much longer it would be before people questioned why we never age."

The tension bled from Draco's shoulders. He had been prepared to offer Tate a life of adventure to explain away a need to leave behind the Aphelion for a while. He should have known Tate would already know his every thought and plan. Draco couldn't hide a thing from Tate.

"So, when will we set out on our next adventure?"

"As soon or as late as you want," Draco answered honestly. "We could retreat from public life and simply enjoy a quiet existence together, or we can travel the world. Perhaps we could visit Cosmos. It's been a while since we saw your friend."

In the blink of an eye, Tate went from sitting at his side to straddling his lap. His face hovered inches from Draco's. Tate's arms wound around Draco's neck. "Hmmm. You tempt me either way. Which should I choose? A life of keeping my sexy husband all to myself or a life of showing him off to the world?"

His gaze moved over Draco's face. Draco felt him searching his mind—like he wanted Draco to know he was there. A smile stretched Tate's lips. "Both, it is."

Draco shook his head. He snagged Tate's ass and hauled him closer. Tiny bat eyes watched them from the shadows—the way they always did. Draco didn't know why the horny horde of new turns hadn't given up hope, but they didn't bother him any longer, and Draco wasn't opposed to giving them a show.

Tate's gaze flickered toward the old iron cage in the corner and near the elevator. The ashes of the vampire who set Tate in Draco's path had blown away nearly a decade ago. Tate still never talked about him or the horrible nightmare he had lived through as a mortal that led him to Draco. Becoming a vampire had healed a part of him mentally, whether he acknowledged it or not. Draco had spent the last decade giving Tate every ounce of love he had been denied as a mortal, and then some. It would never be enough in his eyes.

"You should teach me how to ride a bike."

Draco blinked at the sudden statement. "You don't know how to ride a bike?"

Tate bit his bottom lip, looking slightly ashamed as he shook his head.

Draco held him tighter. "Well, then. I guess we have to move into a quiet neighborhood now. One with safe streets and sidewalks for nighttime bike rides, so Daddy can show you the ropes." Draco toppled onto his back, bringing Tate with him. He snapped his fingers. Their clothes disappeared and a tube of lube appeared in his hand. "First things first. You need to learn balance."

With a giggle, Tate snatched the lube from Draco's hand and went to work wetting his cock. While breathing through his nose, so he wouldn't blow under Tate's expert touch, Draco stared at the night sky. At one time, he thought he might try flying to space as his final resting place. Now, he knew heaven was right here. As Tate's hot tight hole engulfed his cock, Draco knew a happiness and peace that nothing else could give him other than his soulmate. Wherever they went next, they would be the happiest couple, spending this side of eternity together. Forever. Probably with thousands of bats watching. Vampires were perverted like that.

Please consider leaving a review at the retailer where you purchased this book.

Reviews really help with a book's visibility, which allows me to continue writing more stories. Thank you, Charity.

ABOUT THE AUTHOR

CHARITY PARKERSON IS AN award-winning and multi-published author with several companies. Born with no filter from her brain to her mouth, she decided to take this odd quirk and insert it in her characters.

*Eight-time Readers' Favorite Award Winner
*2015 Passionate Plume Award Finalist
*2013 Reviewers' Choice Award Winner
*2012 ARRA Finalist for Favorite Paranormal Romance
*Five-time winner of The Mistress of

the Darkpath

Connect with her online:

*Sign up for her newsletter: https://sen
dfox.com/charityparkerson
*Join her readers' group on Facebook:
http://bit.ly/CharitysTribe
*Website: https://www.charityparkerso
n.com
*A list of her social media accounts and
giveaways all in one place: http://hy.pa
ge/charityparkerson